The Marginals

The Marginals

Nuzhat Hassan

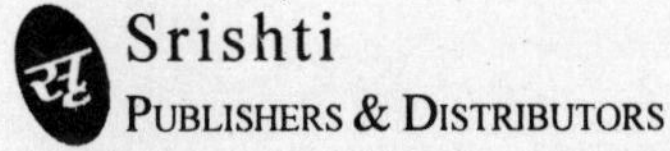

SRISHTI PUBLISHERS & DISTRIBUTORS
64-A, Adhchini
Sri Aurobindo Marg
New Delhi 110 017
srishtipublishers@yahoo.com

First published by SRISHTI PUBLISHERS & DISTRIBUTORS in 2003

Rs. 195.00
ISBN 81-88575-14-3

Typeset in AGaramond 11pt. by Skumar at Srishti

For my mother Birjees.

Dedicated to
Taj
and
Sarmad (Chota Taj).

I acknowledge the Almighty God.

Contents

THE MARGINALS

The margins are that part of the page which is left blank. These margins seem useless to the body of the text yet they define its boundaries.

Society too consists of the mainstream and the margins. Unlike the margins of a page that are static, those of our society are continuously stretching, changing.

Due to the amalgamation that is taking place in society as a fallout of modernization and globalization, the castes and classes that existed have been shaken from centuries of inertia. However, the same society has reorganized itself into the main and the marginals. Probably the need arises since people derive their strength and power by controlling the minds and actions of others. These acts are perpetrated by classifying humans into groups with a certain behavioural pattern. This kind of a classification to my mind helps the mainstream to reduce the threat from such groups to its power and ego.

When the margins are big, those calling the shots are few, the state fascist and the mood intolerant.

On the obverse, when the mainstream is an amalgamation of myriad groups, different from each other, the margins are thin, the divisive lines blurred and the angularities of vision in soft focus.

This is the ideal worth aspiring for and is hopefully within reach.......

THE HUMAN *JALLAD*

It was a day to rejoice. The whole house seemed to be too small to contain the joy of Zubeida, an eighty years old beaming woman. She had been blessed with a grandson – a grandson after ten years of Salim's marriage to Jamila. Ten years is a long time to keep hope burning, but Zubeida had religiously kept the

---

Jallad: Executioner

embers from dying out, her wizened hands preventing the winds of despair from getting at them.

It had not been an easy time but Zubeida seemed to have forgotten it all in her moment of joy – that moment when the baby's first cries announced the arrival to the world of her grandson.

But where was Salim she wondered, wiping her hands on the corner of her frayed dupatta. Where could he be at this momentous moment in his life?

"Salim. Salim. Salim!" she shouted out loud, straining her lungs, oblivious of the limitations of her physique. Her voice echoed down the lanes and made its way beyond the iron gates of the jail. Salim...Salim...Salim.... Where was he? Yes, he was inside. No, he was not a prisoner, yet he was not free either. Salim was a *Jallad*, a man who took lives, a man who was paid for the job legally assigned to him. Salim had taken the lives of so many people that he had lost count.

SALIM. Something hit him between the shoulders. Who had beckoned him? The big burly man turned his shaved head. His pockmarked face with big bulging brown eyes set in pools of red were a shocking sight. His appearance sent an involuntary shiver down the spine. Broad shoulders, immense bulk and the strength of an elephant. He walked aggressively, his whole being suggesting leashed power. Even to the uninitiated, he looked like a bulldozer capable of razing all that was in its way.

Salim had just pulled the handle on another life and now saw what was a part of his existence. A limp corpse, a white envelope – his remuneration – wailing relatives, cursing voices. He walked away, his heavy steps stomping matter-of-factly, crushing all in their wake. All who saw him and his blood shot eyes on such days shied away from him. On his way home, children who played heedlessly in the scorching sun shrank behind trees to let him pass. Men and women, chattering incessantly in the bazaar, would quieten down as if turned to stone.

Salim used to relish this obvious awe that he inspired. He was dreaded! He was like the villain in his favourite Hindi movie. He was the executioner. He was the law. No one dared cross his path. He was the *Jallad*.

But as Salim walked today, his manner was the same but his attitude was not. He no longer relished the silence on the road, nor the awesome fear that he evoked among the folks on the streets. Salim had never thought that his heart would crave for change. Not so very long ago life had been a familiar routine with Jamila and Amma... Till the day Jamila had spoilt it all. She had announced herself to be pregnant about nine months ago. He remembered clearly it was in the month of April last year. Salim could never have thought that Jamila was capable of so devastating him. Yet, in that instant Salim had experienced joy and sorrow, hope and pain, release and enslavement.

That Jamila was pregnant with his child, who would soon enter into this world, had set him thinking of his life. The more he thought, the greater became the burden on his soul. A soul whose existence he had once been unaware of, a soul which he had buried with Raju, the beggar, his only friend, the day he turned into a *Jallad*.

Raju was a drug addict who used to beg. Raju lived in his own world, and had his own vision. Raju was Salim's only friend. Raju used to beg outside the church on a Sunday, Hanuman Mandir on a Tuesday, at the Sai Baba Mandir on a Thursday and outside the mosque on a Friday.

Raju had felt the presence of God at all the places he used to beg and in the hearts of many who used to walk by him. He had felt the presence of the maker on the footpath by his side. He had felt the maker within himself and much beyond. He had never felt his absence anywhere. Raju was the most secular person Salim had come across in his life. Raju used to say things which were beyond the comprehension of Salim but whatever Salim understood and knew he liked.

Raju had his own views on the world. He would often proclaim bitterly that money was the greatest leveller in life. Those who had it and those who did not behaved alike – they all wanted more, more, and more. That Raju was bitter with the ways of people was a well known fact. Often his views were lopsided, or so they seemed to those who surrounded him, yet not many could argue with him.

Raju had his own views on the world. For Raju humans belonged to God, not God to humans. For Raju God did not need any help to turn humans into a faceless, identityless crowd. To Raju humans were far more than the denominations of the currency for which they sold their souls. And Raju found human apathy to all this appalling.

To Raju the bickering of men was meaningless. He found it amusing to watch money move effortlessly from one to the other, with no complaints. He was perpetually surprised that people could not cross over as effortlessly as he did. To Raju, the world was peopled by mad men who ate together, drank together, yet fought each other to annihilate the demon that each was to the other. To Raju the meaninglessness of it all was torture.

Raju used Salim to vent his views, and drugs to escape from them. As the days went by his reliance on drugs increased. When Raju became extremely ill it was unbearable for Salim to see him languish. It was during those days that Amma had told him how the constable had come with work for him; she was very happy that Salim would now be the new *Jallad* following in the footsteps of his father, just as he had followed in the footsteps of *his* father.

All along Salim had been unsure, undecided. However, a long wheezing spell from Raju decided the matter for Salim in an instance. He ran looking for the constable. He ran as though mad dogs were after him. He ran to embrace the life of a *Jallad* and returned to the footpath with the money in a white envelope. Raju was lying limp. Salim turned him over wanting to hand him the envelope hoping against hope that he was not too late. But fate has a treacherous way of its own and the treachery hit Salim when he least expected it. He had sold his soul but his friend was out-of-reach. Salim had cried, and cried and cried inconsolably. A *Jallad* crying? Strange are the ways of life. Stranger indeed than fiction it is said.

As time passed, Salim became a regular *Jallad* with all the trappings in place. Yet today Salim's soul had dared to rear its head again and had proclaimed an existence beyond his reach. All these years Salim had let the wails of relatives and their curses fall on deaf ears but now his soul was making him edgy.

He, Salim the *Jallad*, was the visible symbol, the butt of hatred, the man in the eye of the storm of the volley of curses that relatives rained on him as he moved past the iron gates. He was cursed for the act of snuffing lives by mothers and wives, brothers and children. He, who till now had never regretted them but had learnt to relish them, was now feeling uncomfortable. Why the hell didn't they curse the police, the judge? Why in heaven's name was he being held responsible for the acts of others? Why, indeed.

Day after day the irksome ritual crystallized into painful reality. Salim would crouch on his bed, hiding from the police constable who earlier used to be the welcome harbinger of work, trying hard to wish away the reality of life which was overwhelming him. The reality of life....

His child would be forced to follow in his father's footsteps just as he had unwittingly walked in his father's and had continued to walk till this stage in life. But how could he say no to the police? He was the only *Jallad* around. Who would bring justice if he refused? Not everybody could pull the handle. It needed a *Jallad* to do that.

All was well till he had heard about his impeding fatherhood. His thoughts, his pain, his destiny would have survived only till his last breath but now he was not so sure. Why, O lord, was he being traumatised? He was certain that life would play the same old treacherous tricks egged on by those around, forcing the role of a human butcher on his child.

Yet, Salim secretly nourished a ray of hope. He prayed to God, fervently, five times a day… and five times a day he prayed for a daughter. A daughter whom he would marry off to a respectable man far away – far away from here. So far away that the wails and curses surrounding him would never reach her. He willed himself into believing this fantasy and so nine months passed and life continued …. turbulent within yet not enough to ruffle the exterior.

Salim strode into his house to see the overjoyed Zubeida. Zubeida turned to see her son, Salim, the joy in her life, whom she had wanted to tell the news she had been bursting with all morning. Oh! How her son would dance with gay abandon!

"Salim," she whispered, "you have been blessed

with a son. Salim do you hear me? Salim.... Salim...."

Salim stood like a rock. His mother's words had shattered the semi stupor in which he had sought comfort all these months.

Salim could hear the echo of his feet and the crank of the handle stretch beyond his lifetime. Yes, fate had tricked him again.

This was how he turned into stone. This was how the curses resounded in his body. This was how he was when somebody tapped him on the shoulder.

It was the jailer, with a box of sweets in his hand and a broad grin on his face.

SHADES OF LIFE

The day was bright and sunny. It had rained through the night and the earthy smells filled the nostrils. The lazy town was humming with activity charged by the fresh, cool breeze. Yet, Sheila sat under the mango tree, half dead to the vibrant world around. She was oblivious of the gay buzz of the bees, of the mowing of cows and of the youthful chatter of Meena.

Sheila had slipped quietly into a reverie. Her life had been full of contradictions. She could see clearly, even now after so many years, the palatial house lit up brightly, full of people bustling about. She could hear the sound of drums, which announced the festivities. It was as though they synchronized their beat with her steps and heartbeat. Her heart, she remembered, had beaten louder than the drums.

How far away it was, years ago, when she had glimpsed this house for the first time, amidst the teasing chatter of the bridesmaids. Sheila had been a young, demure, beautiful bride.

Life had held many promises then but slowly, each day and every year had unfolded to the mixed memories which were her only companions besides young Meena.

Like the dappled shade of the mango tree, she too had lived all shades of life. From the early days of excitement and plenty to the present stage of penury, from wifehood to widowhood, from life to living hell.

She had moved on with life but had never been able to comprehend why she had been singled out for such treatment. Over the years, with age and experience, she had begun to accept the hand life had dealt her. Unwillingly, at first. But, at last, she clearly understood that however much she may rave or rant, she would still have to live through her lot.

Sheila continued to ponder why fate had dealt her such a lousy hand. She recalled clearly the manner in which her son and daughter-in-law had craved for a child. They had gone to shrines of various faiths and religions in their quest for an heir. Often, Sheila who had also celebrated the birth of Meena, her grand-daughter, had wondered whether her existence was a mere mockery of the fulfillment of the insistent prayers of her son and daughter-in-law.

Meena was an unfortunate child. Her parents had died when she was only two years old, leaving her helpless in the lap of her only hope – Sheila. Yes, it is said that God knows best, but sometimes humans try all means to twist destiny only to be slapped in the face.

Meena, now a girl of sixteen, was Sheila's biggest sorrow. Sheila had lived through the death of all her near and dear ones in a string of unfortunate incidents, but it was Meena's existence which, day after day, year after year engulfed her.

Not far away in Mirzapur there lived a young man called Kalu. Kalu was a complete businessman for whom money was all important. The only thing that affected him deeply was his business. This very day young Kalu, in contrast to Sheila, was full of hope and anticipation. He had just hit the jackpot. Years of hard labour had finally been rewarded. He had been nominated to run the agency of a reputed firm in the town. His joy knew no bounds and his mind was so preoccupied in calculating the profits that would be his that even his sleep was getting affected.

Kalu was a young man, only thirty years of age, yet he was quite worldly wise. Life had not been easy for him. After the death of his father, he had grown overnight from a mere child into an adult. He could have gone the way most do – being cynical, cursing fate and wallowing in self-pity. To his credit he had not let his personal tragedy spill over and swamp his self. He had long ago learnt to get up after a fall, dust his clothes and walk on. Somehow he had mastered the art of dictating his own fate. Those around him envied him, some even hated him, but none could better him at the things he did. For, Kalu had never left things to chance or destiny.

For him, even destiny waited, and seemed to love following his broad shouldered physique to achievement after achievement.

Kalu had learnt another important lesson in life. And that was never to rest on his laurels. His whole being signified movement. Faster and forward. Better and better. At thirty and single, he had never really thought of the other facets of being, those dimensions of life which if neglected lead to an awkward personality, ill fitted into the designs of nature. For Kalu, the biggest fear was that of going without food, clothing and shelter. His experiences with life had almost snapped his balance in this regard. His fear, which was real at one stage, was now leading him on and on and on on the road to accumulate millions without a thought as to why he needed them.

Need, if unlimited, leads to desire and desire, when unbridled, produces monsters. But, where was the need for Kalu to think of all this, to think of his purpose in the world.

A river, when young, rushes through the mountains, blissfully unaware of what lies ahead. Crashing down, racing gaily, accumulating all that comes in its way, reducing it to dust. It is only when its flow slows down does it have to let go and deposit its accumulated wealth by its banks for those whom it never really thought of, for those whom it never really knew, before finally merging with the ocean, traceless.

Kalu's car finally reached the small town of Hamirpur. He got out and walked into the premises rented by his men, men who stood obsequiously around. These men were roughly of his own age, but that is where the similarity ended. While they were with him, they felt insignificant and resorted to all modes of sycophancy to catch Kalu's attention.

Bhura pointed out the various rooms, as he filled Kalu in with the details of the bungalow, an elegant white colonial building, from where men of the Raj had run the show. For an instant, Kalu felt like a Maharaja, a man whose word was law.

Bhura, Nathu, Mangu, Munna were all vying with each other to impress Kalu with the details of the plan they had worked out to run the agency. Kalu said nothing but smiled in his heart. What differentiated him from this riffraff for whom he was lord and master, was his ability to get results and achieve success. For Kalu morals were merely a distraction, at most having some historical importance. What mattered was results – whatever the means. Luckily for him, the total degeneration in the fabric of society had helped him keep his overhead costs low and yet come out trumps. He had fit cleanly in the mould of a success – as defined by the society in which he lived.

Sheila a stony figure was still lost in her own world when something stirred within, slowly yet surely as she became aware of the milkman speaking to Meena.

Meena was unaware of the thoughts passing through her grandmother's mind. In fact, mistaking her to be fast asleep, she had taken the opportunity to speak to Ranvir, the milkman.

Meena's chattering, even if on mundane issues, gnawed at Sheila's heart like a saw rasping on wood.

She strained her ears to listen to what Meena was saying to the milkman. As she understood the conversation her stony visage turned pale with fear and terror. How dare Ranvir suggest to the girl that she was capable of making money and he could help her do it. Meena, the idiot, was pestering him to tell her how. Ranvir, with a lewd laugh, slyly told her to meet him in the park in the evening and he would tell her all.

Sheila's ears burnt. She of royal lineage, had to hear all this too. O God! What else would life unfold. Her granddaughter would turn into a prostitute right under her nose? No. No,...No,...the word beat louder than the sound of drums had in her ears. Her whole being shook with rage. That moment of shock and realization snapped the false sense of pride which had never let her venture out of her house to seek help. Never would she let this happen.

Sheila called Meena sharply, got up and walked up to the house. She walked inside and took out a tattered pension form from under her mattress. She firmly told Meena to lock the door and like a woman possessed with a mission walked out of the house. On the way she met Ranoo, Ranvir's wife, and told her clearly what she had overheard and threatened her and Ranvir with dire action if they ever looked Meena's way again. Her words seemed to impact a shocked Ranoo. Royalty, it seemed, still had currency, even in penury.

Then Sheila hobbled a long way down the road, to the elegant bungalow she knew had housed the D.M.'s office.

Outside the white bungalow sat Bhura. Sheila, approached him and pushed the form towards him. "Fill it," she ordered, with such commanding clarity that surprised her decayed frame. Bhura, used to being commanded, was in a playful obliging mood. He humoured this caricature of a woman and started to fill the form.

About half an hour later Kalu, who came from within, was amused by the scene in front of him. Bhura was trying to fill a form, while an old woman sat on the steps besides him. She was unable to answer most of the items and Bhura, who was now at pains to get her out of his hair, was becoming impatient.

Kalu, the leader, walked up to Bhura and took the form from him. As he glanced through what Bhura had written, a long forgotten, yet very familiar vision of a very small boy leapt before him. A boy who was small and fatherless, who had grown overnight from a child to an adult. His heart swam with emotions of helplessness and the fear of insecurity. Insecurity of food, of shelter, of clothing, of self-respect.

In that instant Kalu could feel the anguish of this woman as he could his own. He could also feel her helplessness and more. An unknown strange urge to reach out to this woman engulfed him threatening to drown him. He wanted to cry out, he wanted to hurl abuses at destiny's dictator. Luckily, he regained balance before any such thing happened. Gently he took the woman by her hand. He led her to the waiting area. He asked her what amount she wanted as pension. Kalu then fixed her "pension" to be delivered at her door by Bhura on the 22nd of each month even as he wiped a tear, which threatened to spill from his eye.

And so Kalu, who had never thought of the finer emotions of life and who had believed that nothing could change him and his ways was thus transformed by a frail unknown old woman, from a mere businessman to a human being.

OF FETTERS AND FREEDOM

The festival season had begun. The monsoon had come and gone. The fields were well taken care of. The people had lots of time on their hands and most of them had nothing to do except while it away. The villagers played cards, heard the radio play songs and gossiped after they had exhausted all forms of amusement.

In this backdrop one fine day the gypsies arrived. Their dust laden bullock carts creaked to a halt on the outskirts of the town. They quickly piled out from their shelters and took over the barren patch of land which belonged to the Gram Sabha.

Most of them were busy with themselves; children wailed, mothers fretted, fathers unloaded carts as the old folks chatted. Only Mansi, vibrant with life, flitted from one group to the other till she had met and interacted with all her peers.

Mansi's father, Harbir, the Pradhan, was a proud old man who watched his youngest child indulgently. She had the ability to twist him around her little finger with unmatched ease. He had many children, so many that he could not recall the names of most of them. Most of his children had taken up work in the big cities. He had lost touch with them slowly over the years due to his wandering ways.

Harbir felt a silent joy as he watched Mansi. Her

slight frame and beauty was a reassurance for him. He would not have to exert much to find a suitable match for her, he thought.

Unaware of the thoughts in her father's mind Mansi was playing with the cows, rubbing their heads affectionately as the sun dipped towards the horizon, wrapping up its long rays on his way back home. The scene was a picture of bliss. Peace descended on the camp as the stars put up their regular show in the firmament. Mansi lay open-eyed gazing at the stars till sleep overtook her preoccupation with them.

The stars shone brightly as the moon played hide and seek behind the clouds. The cool breeze, laden with the fragrance of blossoms on the trees, touched Mansi's cheeks as it too was captivated by her charm and grace just as all those who beheld her were entranced. Her big eyes spoke a language of their own. Everyone and everything that came within her orbit was spellbound by her unselfconscious charm.

Mansi was a lanky girl, a gypsy by birth, and a sensitive human being. She had been a naughty, playful child. She was all that girls her age ought to be and more. Yet to the men, women and children of the town she was merely a gypsy.

To Mansi, as yet untouched by the definitions that life imposed on people and their actions, she was simply a young girl who had a lot of expectations from life and many aspirations to fulfill. Mansi was life itself, not willing to be bound down, not willing to take things at face value. The age at which she stood gave a fire to her expectations and an aggression to her being. The age at which she stood made her ready for flight on as yet untested wings – a dangerous prospect yet a reality we all encounter. Some have their flight to safety, some develop snags even before they take off…

The indulgent father was unaware of the subtle changes that Mansi was experiencing physically and emotionally but not so her mother, a shrewd woman who was a hawk in matters concerning her brood. She was a true gypsy woman at heart and knew that a girl like Mansi was capable of raising quite a storm. The experiences that she had had all her life had taught her ample truths about life and living.

She had learnt the bitter way that her tribe was looked down upon by the society around. She knew that they were treated as a criminal tribe, and worse the women were all seen as having loose morals.

She had learnt to hate that society. The society whose respectable men looked with open lust at all and sundry while passing by. The society whose women were caged by tradition to keep them away from sin. It was a society which needed restrictions to be able to enjoy freedom.

And they? They were free – free as the birds, free as the wind, free as the rays of the sun. Free yet never straying from their destination. The society she held in utter contempt was proud and peculiar. Full of double standards, full of flaws. Full of the worst show of the devil – where there was no freedom of thought or speech. It was a society where what was said was different from what was meant or thought; where each survived by pulling down the other.

She stretched on her bed under the tattered tent. She was a gypsy and proud of the fact. She knew that truth to be valued has to be arrived at through experience. She knew and saw a lot around her. But what worried her at the moment was what she saw and felt about Mansi.

Mansi was still only a child. A child about to take wing, a child who would fly soon. It was a time to be careful of the vultures all around but Mansi was becoming more and more carefree. Her mother was not worried about those in the camp. They were all folks worthy of trust. It was those who slithered outside, ready to strike, that she would have to watch out for.

The sleepy town, parched for sources of entertainment, soon heard that the gypsies had set up camp and a wave of excitement rippled through it. Almost everybody knew about them by the afternoon, and by the evening the police had received instructions from the young and very propah Captaan Saab to keep a strict eye on the camp. He did not want the gypsies to create any unpleasantness around.

The young Captaan and his wife were more English than the British thought Sher Singh, the Station House Officer, who had seen many changes in his lifetime. At his stage and station in life he could ill afford to ignore his Saab's instructions, or, for that matter, voice his personal opinions. So, he dispatched a young and smart police constable to patrol around the camp on a bike.

A bike raises quite a bit of dust at the best of times. But in this sleepy town a bike carrying a constable heading towards the gypsy camp had an electric effect. All kinds of rumors were initiated and/or passed on by word of mouth, so much so that by nightfall many people collapsed due to over exertion of mind and mouth.

Young Veer Singh, the dedicated police Constable, took his job seriously and kept a watch, day in and day out, on the activities of the gypsies. He moved around with the men and mingled with the boys to collect intelligence. He wanted to prove his worth to the Saab and he slogged very hard. There were times when he felt like a gypsy himself, so involved was he in the project.

Yet, Veer Singh was not happy with his progress. The number of petty crimes had gone up in the town and Sher Singh had conveyed Captaan Saab's displeasure to Veer Singh for his failure in preventing the gypsies from committing them.

Veer Singh fretted and fumed. He was becoming aware of how he had been trapped into this assignment. He was the scapegoat for the inefficiency of the whole Police Station; he was to pay the price for the inactivity of his colleagues and seniors who were allowing the small time criminals in town to have a field day. He was suffering for their inaction as the theory that the gypsies were committing the crimes had gained ground. It was enough to show him up in very poor light.

Veer Singh became aware of how vulnerable he was. If the thefts and robberies did not stop, and if the innocent gypsies were not fixed by him as the culprits, he would face a gloomy future. No doubt it would be marred by suspensions and enquiries.

At dawn Veer Singh sat gloomily staring with unseeing eyes at the dusty motorcycle in front of him. Life seemed hopeless. He felt he was a misfit in the force. Moreover, he was hopelessly raw. He could see the snigger on the faces of his colleagues if they should hear about his state today.

No, Veer Singh decided. He would rather die than allow this to happen. He would not let Sher Singh do him in.

Meanwhile, Sher Singh sat comfortably in the Thana grinning from ear to ear. He was well aware of Veer Singh's predicament. Veer Singh had deserved all he was undergoing. In nominating Veer Singh, the promising fresh outspoken lad who has recently reported to the Police Station, Sher Singh had not really favoured him. In one master stroke, he had ensured certain doom for Veer Singh of course with the silent acquiescence of the others.

Veer Singh thought and thought until slowly a glimmer of understanding dawned upon him. He would stymie Sher Singh he promised himself. He drew up a plan to enlist the help of…who else but Harbir to put a few fellows behind bars.

Harbir was unaware of the trap being laid by this handsome lad, this lad who spoke with sincerity and who had a particular way with words. The same lad who had befriended Harbir and won him over with a few bottles of rum. Slowly, he had preyed upon Harbir's ambition of dying as a pradhan by insinuating he might be supplanted. He spun stories about the political aspirations of Ranvir and Sukhvir, who were the sons of his closest rival. After the death of their father, Ranvir and Sukhvir had emotionally declared that they would never rest in peace till they fulfilled their father's unfinished tasks. Harbir had never taken their threats seriously as they had seemed more of an emotional outburst.

However, now as Veer Singh fabricated details of non-existent secretive goings on, Harbir was no longer so sure. Veer Singh had conjured up plausible stories, laced with part reality, to convince both Harbir and his wife.

The rum worked for Harbir, but his wife, the shrewd gypsy woman, was not to be won over so easily. In fact she, always suspicious, proved to be a big thorn for Veer Singh. He had seen many dominating women but none quite like her. Harbir, whether drunk or sober, was used to following her dictates without a whimper and she was proving to be a big drain on Veer Singh's resources. Often, just as Harbir was adequately drunk, and in a state molten enough to be moulded, she would appear from nowhere to shout and curse them both and drag Harbir out of reach.

Veer Singh clenched his hand for the hundredth time wondering what he could possibly do. Just as he had lost all hope an opportunity presented itself. O why had he not seen it before? He chided himself for his foolishness. He had allowed his own problems to affect his thinking or else he could never have missed such a possibility. The opportunity came to him in the form of an impressionable young girl called Mansi.

Veer Singh unclenched his hand, smiled a winning smile and stroked his hair in the only way he knew.

The way popular heroes did in Hindi movies to impress the heroines.

But Veer Singh was out of luck. He was left stroking his head, while Mansi, busy with her own thoughts and deeply engrossed with herself, failed to notice him at all. She ran into her tent followed by a yapping dog who even had the cheek to growl at him.

Veer Singh remained rooted to the ground, his mind busy changing strategies. He had to win over this threesome if he was to achieve the glory he pined for. The mere thought of it expanded his chest at least five inches more than what it normally was.

It was then, in that moment of extreme concentration, that he hit upon a plan that would have even left the Captaan grinning from ear to ear, to say nothing of Sher Singh.

The next morning, at the break of dawn, Veer Singh arrived at Harbir's doorstep with a big bag full of goodies and a lot to gossip about. Within ear shot of the protective shrew, he spoke to Harbir about how Bholu had made lewd remarks about Mansi. Veer Singh smiled inwardly as he saw from the corner of his eye that the woman had made a rapid movement on hearing his statement. His strategy had just begun to work.

Slowly but surely he used his poison tongue to paint make-believe pictures in front of the doting parents playing on their only fear – their paranoia about Mansi.

Harbir, who was no longer young, became worried. His dim eyes and failing health added colours of doom to the pictures painted by Veer Singh. His wife's preoccupation with Mansi's well-being led her into believing the horrible stories. And over the days and nights both Harbir and his wife were saddened by the load they carried in their minds. They wondered what they could do, and they planned how they could get rid of those ruffians

Bholu, Chunna, Mangal, etc. Harbir had often reprimanded these lads for their immature ways. They had always laughed off Harbir's concern and he had a very poor opinion about them.

Just when their problems seemed so unsurmountable, Veer Singh appeared on their doorstep, a spring in his walk and a song on his lips.

He enquired after the health of Harbir and his family and sat down silently. The awkward silence was broken by the woman. She told him about her fears. She told him how she had seen Bholu watching Mansi. She also told him she was sure Chunna had been peeping into her tent.

Veer Singh laughed a bitter laugh. He could smell success. He had managed to twist these unsuspecting folks around his little finger. It just needed a little push and the matter would be concluded neatly.

23rd February 1954. He would never forget the date. It was on this day that he had received a commendation from the Inspector General for his exemplary work on the gypsies.

Now with those boys firmly in jail and the gypsies out of his hair, he walked a tall man amongst his companions. With the change in Veer Singh's fortune, Sher Singh also changed colours in the true style of a seasoned policeman. He looked at him with joy. Captaan Saab was happy at the vindication of his orders. That night Veer Singh had slept a relieved man. He had tasted the joy of recognition. Moreover, how did it matter whether these boys were guilty or not? Those ruffians would have got themselves into some problem sooner or later. They might even have murdered somebody.... They had been saved from a darker destiny by him, Constable Veer Singh!

In deep slumber, he smiled, a satisfied man. Life's promises seemed very much within his reach.

Veer Singh was destined to wear many medals in the

long years of service but the commendation he had received for apprehending the gypsies held special value for it heralded the beginning of the rise.

HEERA, THE HIJRA

Heera, Bano, Chameli and Bela lived in the interior of the city amongst such squalor that the uninitiated eye would easily dismiss them as beggars. On taking a closer look, it would be apparent that they were a strange breed and not beggars. They were neither male nor female. They were hijras*.

---

*Hijra: Eunuch

Hijras. The word throws up pictures as varied as the colours of the rainbow. Foul–mouthed, betel chewing obnoxious characters who move around to extort money on every occasion from the money-clutching middle class. Their methods are many. They dance and they sing, they cajole and they threaten, they beg and they extort.

Do they? One look at the four huddled forms would dismiss these thoughts out of any mind with a modicum of sense.

A straight figure moved towards the foursome stealthily. She had a lot to say and caused a terrible outburst amongst them. They seemed to lose all their balance. They began screaming and shouting and uttering foul abuses.

The old hag Heera was the first to regain balance as she let go of Chameli's hair. Chameli kicked Bela fiercely. Bela shouted and cursed. Curses laden with abuses of the kind one does not hear even in the brothels.

Amazed and intrigued, I moved closer to them. By now the straight figure had disappeared and with her, like magic, disappeared the discord.

What was it that the lonely figure had said? Why did they turn from calm to vicious to calm within moments. I had to find out. My quick pace was arrested by one leering look from Chameli. My resolve to find out also suffered a jolt. I turned in my tracks, threw away my half smoked cigarette and walked, unknowing steps, till I reached the park nearby. I slunk down onto a bench. The faces of these hijras – calm an instant, vicious in another and calm again – were a photographer's delight. But what intrigued me today was not their photogenic appeal but their human tragedy.

I had never before come so close to hijras. Yes, I had seen them dancing and prancing about in the neighbourhood, beating drums, jumping around. I had dismissed them in those moments as – well, those hijras. Today was different. Today I had come closer to them, seeing them for the first time as humans. I walked away slowly from the locality with heavy steps. I wanted to quell the familiar throbbing in my head. I knew this was not the end of the matter. I knew my curiosity would force me to find out more as always.

As I moved away from the bench, my thoughts overwhelmed me. I, Karan, am a well-known journalist. This introduction brings a wry smile to my face. Well known indeed. I have worked hard exposing scams and film rolls. People have appreciated my initiative. For want of competition I have grown into a celebrity. In my heart I am a culprit. I feel like a pimp. Feeding on people's sorrows like a vulture feeding on a carcass. When I shot my now famous documentary on the drought in Rajasthan and sold it for a handsome sum, something in me died. I felt a deep revulsion against the business I had made of human tragedy. But the fact is in real life sorrow sells. Happiness doesn't. I needed the money.

Today editors surround me. Interviewers shadow

me. A celebrity has to fit the bill. I am doing a remarkable job. Today I have again left many speechless. The bureaucrats pamper me. The politicians dread me. The people read me. I am Karan the well known journalist. Day has turned to night. I have retired from the world of make-believe. I am about to fall asleep. In my mind's eye I see the unedited version of the scene with the hijras. I was sure this would come back to haunt me, but so soon? I would have to do something to rectify my photographic memory. Pain needs no replay. Once is enough.

The place I live in is akin to a luxurious hotel. A place to come and go. A place full of all gadgets made to fulfil human greed in the name of luxury.

I picked up the phone and called Lachhu my contact who had links of all sorts. I told him I wanted to do a programme on hijras. I told him I needed material. I told him I wanted the backdrop of the city. I told him I was ready to pay. I could almost hear Lachhu the creep smile as he heard the urgency in my voice. Obviously it held the promise of pots of gold.

Lachhu came to see me in the morning with one big burly hijra in tow. One signal from him and she started off, as if displaying her wares, about all those whom she could summon. When I asked about the old hijras who have a dera in the city, her face seemed to fall a bit. She said dismissively, " Old hags! Who bothers about them except some chelas? You want hijras for a film, I will give you as many as you want." One look of disgust from me, which held the threat of loss of business for Lachhu, made him signal to her to stop.

I was obsessed. I had to meet the four who had captured my mind in those moments forever. I told Lachhu what I wanted. I put a wad of notes on the table and walked away leaving them to tie up the nitty-gritty. Lacchu now got his act into motion. I returned after half an hour to find the thin ramrod structure in front of me. How did they find her? The one capable of inciting the foursome into a shameless dance, a vicious orgy of abuses and fisticuffs.

The thin one looks like a hawk. Her emaciated body gives off a revolting stench. It seems she has not had a bath for days. She is tongue-tied. She emits a wail: Why has burra saab bought her here, she questions. She is an old hag to be pitied. She is a useless person now to all around. She wipes unshed tears from her cheeks and shuffles as if to move off. Lachhu crosses her path aggressively.

I intervene sweet-tongued. She is absolutely essential in my designs to find out about hijras in general and those four in particular. She was a shrewd one, she did not budge. She kept moaning and groaning, chanting and roaming. Pleading one instant, threatening another. Frustrated, I wanted to shout at her. But, knowing better, I ran my hand through my hair and tugged at it. I was caught once again, a victim of my curiosity. Why do I bother, why indeed? Why couldn't the tension building up in me resolve without my having to go through these tortures again and again.

But, no. This is the way I was. The tensions and the knots within would work their way to their logical conclusion. Logical? Conclusion? I shook my head as I looked at the form in front of me. Neither male nor female, but human. As human as you and me.....Yes. As human as you and me. The thought was strangely revolting as well as comforting. Neither head nor toe, neither beginning nor end. We all come forth from the unknown taking forms beyond our control. We all go back to the unknown, unfathomable leaving behind those forms we learnt to call our own.

This body, which we all learn to love before we can love anything else, laughs mockingly at the foolishness of its worship. It is pampered, it is oiled, it is draped, it is perfumed as long as alive. It stinks, it reeks, it decays, it burns, it disintegrates with a certainty we all know well.

At last she spoke, "My name is Rekha, I was the most beautiful hijra around. Those four hijras you saw are my chelas. Unfortunately, with the disappearance of nawabs and zamindars, we have been reduced to this plight. In days gone by, hijras commanded respect in society. Not all could afford the luxury of keeping a hijra. A hijra was strong enough to work from morning to night yet safe to trust with your wife." She laughed out loud and then continued. "The tragedy is men are used to mistrusting those they lock back home while they roam freely on the roads. Freedom is the keep of the fittest, the strongest. Might has always been right….."

She is tricking me. She is tricking me, the shrewd wretch. She has read me like a book. She knows I will not let her off till she tells me the story. So she has started reeling untruths – the untruths she knows the likes of me believe in. I gave in, gave in for the moment to the smart eunuch for whom I was beginning to feel something akin to respect.

She babbled on, in typical fashion. I listened bemused. After her act, she got up, bowed and waited for permission to be dismissed. I entered into my role. I waved my hand to indicate her release. She jumped, turned around and walked away not even waiting to squabble for remuneration. Yet it was in her movements, in her gait, in her manner that I read dismissal – utter and complete. Dismissal of me and my likes. I felt a shame, a contempt for my own self grow within me. I felt a sinking of my esteem in my very own eyes.

I moved physically, trying to move away from my feelings. I went inside, I dressed in style for the luncheon meeting scheduled an hour later in the high class hotel across the road. I was to meet the who's who of the press and even for a celebrity like me these engagements were necessary for survival. Like the salt in the pickle, like the balm on the mummies, like the naphthalene in the woollens, these meetings were mandatory for us. Till our faces appeared in the pages of the dailies, till we were seen and heard, what were we?

Life moved in circles but my mind loved tangents. The ramrod structure provided the spark. I moved away from my image in the mirror. I moved away from the shadows into light. I threw off my elegant clothes. I removed my adornments as I switched to reality. The reality of the hijras. I, Karan, a well known journalist, had made up my mind to tackle them on my own.

I walked once again, walked and walked to the place where all this had started. Finally, I reached the spot which reeked of extreme poverty and helplessness.

I waited by the side of the road. Nothing interesting. I waited till evening. No sign. I went away. I came again. Days passed. My beard grew, my presence in the neighbourhood became familiar. To exist for hours and days, I had to pass the time, I had to stick to those around and slowly I learnt to merge with them.

Finally, life afforded a scintillating opportunity. Satya, the local dada, started on the topic of Heera. I became all ears, my being tingled with expectation, but I willed my manner to remain unruffled. I listened casually. He informed us that those vermin had not been seen for so many days that it was quite extraordinary. What could have scared them off, he speculated. What indeed. Specially when any number of threats and abuses from the local dadas had not. I kicked myself hard in my mind. How could I have been so foolish. Did I scare them off? And why? What had I done?

The mystery deepened the restlessness of my mind. Was I the cause? The cause....My nervous mind sensed failure. Failure of Mission Hijra.

I gave up the day's work. I was too disturbed. I walked away with heavy footsteps, I walked senseless –

all mind no body, all thought no feelings. I walked. I walked many miles. People on footpaths heckled, rickshaw pullers shouted but I still walked senseless.

Finally, tired, the body gave up and I fell in a heap on the footpath by the bus stand. I closed my eyes. Then I could feel, or rather sense, the hijras in front of me. Through half open eyelids I could see the foursome, huddled in a corner, hush–hushing each other, looking with curious glances at one and all. They took me for a beggar. They huddled in the dark behind the bus stand. Fate had been kind. This was a coincidence divine. That which I had hunted for all over in known places, I found here in a senseless state. I laughed a mirthless laugh. I, Karan, the well known journalist, a beggar, sharing a footpath with hijras! I laughed aloud involuntarily a bitter laugh. Heera cursed the others in undertones. The four chelas seemed worried. I strained my ears to hear. Heera began chanting...weird unintelligible chants which became meaningful when pieced together.

She was cursing the fate which had given them such long lives; she was bitter with each and everyone. Imagine, she said, they could have led normal lives but for that wretched woman. She was threatening them to get hold of new robust chelas or face expulsion. Expulsion? From where? Aren't we already expelled? Expelled from each side, living on the edge? How can we condemn others who do not deserve such a fate into the hands of the wretch. Yes, we too have morals, we too have to face the maker. The maker who made us so in his wisdom. We do not question it, we accept it...yet he made us so.

What the world made of us is for the world to answer. For our deeds we have to answer. Expel us all you want but I, Heera, will never...never sell myself so. A bitter laugh escaped her dry lips. Chameli was aghast. She tried to shut her up. Bela was weeping softly while Bano looked around suspiciously.

And what if we do not do her bidding. She will beat us and kill us. Worse still she will bury us alive.

She has all those powers over us since we are her chelas. She and the rest will hunt us down. They will bribe their way through to find us. And after finding us...they will force us to do their bidding...some young fellow will die to be reborn a hijra.

O Lord! forgive us. Show us the way...they moaned.

The chowkidar hushed them with one blow of his lathi. They cowered. Pulled their pallus over their faces wanting to hide behind the cloth in an attempt to run away from their misfortune.

Bela wept and moaned, "Why don't we buy peace and do as told. We are duty bound to obey – the Lord knows. Why not do what someone else would anyway? Why suffer such misfortune?"

"No," shrieked Heera as if possessed. "No! I will fight to the last. Think...think of the time you were recast. Have you forgotten the pain, the sorrow, the remorse? Have you forgotten what it takes to lose the love, the joy, the identity?"

Yes, Bela knew she was right, but Bela did not like to suffer. Bela did not want to live huddled in ditches and drains when she could lead a normal life with chelas around. Yes, there was pain, there was sorrow. But time cured things, cured so that the community lived, loved and survived. If not they, someone would do the needful to carry the baton forward so why not them? Why not them, indeed. Why should she suffer for the sake of Heera?

She got up, dusted her clothes and ran away speedily. Before Heera knew what was happening Chameli and Bano had also run away from her. Heera was left alone. Pain in her eyes, her stony eyes. Waiting for the obvious. She would not see the light of day. The wretch would find her. There was no use running away. She had been abandoned by those whom she had considered family. She felt the pain surge in her chest, she felt the sorrow, the humiliation, the abuse someone somewhere would be forced to feel. The world would soon change for someone somewhere whom she had tried to save, someone somewhere whom she wanted to save. She howled with pain, she cried out loud. Her cries touched the human in me. I woke up to her plight. She changed from a character in my story to a wretched being suffering in front of me.

I shook myself. I awoke to the present. I the journalist, would love to watch till the story's end and reproduce it – sell it – make money, attend seminars – talk of a enunch's plight. I, the human, would love to help her, save her, take her home, protect her. I, Karan, was split between I the human and I the journalist. I watched my two identities quarrel. I watched each present its case. I watched till the chowkidar's lathi struck a tight blow on my head. I lay one eye open, the other shut, waiting for the time to pass, waiting...waiting. Senseless.

I returned to my senses midday. I was still sprawled

on the footpath. There was no sign of Heera anywhere. I looked all over, I tried to separate dream from reality. I tried to tell myself it was all a dream. I tried to cry. I tried to assure myself that Heera was still alive. I tried to wish myself elsewhere. My hand reached my head to tug at my hair.... It touched the bump and myth and reality fell into place. A picture emerged of me, Karan, who had let time slip out of his hand, who could have done much...but who did nothing.

The fire that had possessed Heera, the fire of purpose, had long died inside me. It took Heera to make me realize a lot about myself. Each situation throws up choices, failing to grasp either reduces even me, Karan, to a *Napunsak* – a hijra.

I slowly moved back to familiar surroundings. I tried to regain myself. I, Karan, returned with great force to my life, the life of a journalist. I retrained my thoughts. I dressed my body, I emptied my mind. I drank myself out of my senses. Yet all along Heera haunted me – the old hag with a foul mouth and a heart of gold...The old hag with a mission, a purpose. The old hag who had managed to hold a mirror to my soul. I crushed my cigarette between my fingers. I tried to crush the helplessness within. I got up and walked once again to the place where everything had started.

I went to the same old square whose angularities were clearly etched in my mind. I saw the threesome happily there. A photo of Heera mocked at me, incense burning by its side.

I walked away. Far away. The scene kept drumming in my head. I walked away yet again...I wish I had walked in time....

Life returned to outward normalcy with time. I wrote volumes on misery. I wrote volumes on courage. I wrote and I wrote with Heera still in my head. I then sat and confronted her, talked to her, asked her why she haunted me so. Heera's stony eyes turned tearful, her manner became morose. Karan, she said, I died. It was probably destined – but I died once. You and your kind die a thousand deaths before time. You who have the power do not exercise it when you should, when you can. Your courage is locked away covered under layers and layers of selfishness, of pride, of ego, of lack of confidence. If you, Karan, failed to act in time, each time, of what use is your ability? Of what use is your pride?

I hung my head in shame. The thoughts in my bosom had taken form through Heera and mocked me.

I picked myself up from the familiar safe surroundings and walked and walked and walked...I crushed my cigarette, I cried, I cried and I cried.

I looked at myself, a well known journalist saw a suffering human being. A successful person saw a weak imprisoned soul, wanting to break free from the cage of labels, from the cage of illusions. I saw my lifeless form look at me with hope dying in its eyes. I felt for it as I had learnt to feel for Heera. This time I would not let go, this once I would act in time.

In that moment of deep realization, my heart began to flutter with hope. The being responded to the call of existence and I have travelled the road from being a successful person to a fulfilled one. And from the dark dungeons of misery I have travelled to bliss.

What have I lost? What have I gained? No longer do these questions hold any meaning, no longer any weight. I now write what I see, I now do as I feel. I still live, I still earn, I still rejoice. Truth exists all around and within. Acknowledge it. . .Acknowledge it.

THE LEPERS

Early morning. Nariman Point. The sea haughty, withdrawn. The mind eager, receptive. The crunch of shoes, the joy inside. The sight of handsome young bodies a reminder of the creator sublime. The turning sharp. The voices monotonous. Lepers begging, a routine expected occurrence. The clanging of coins. Metal on metal. The decay, the rot, the dripping features of the huddled forms by the side underscore the hurried steps, the withdrawn features, the haughty gait of the wealthy seth.

The differences too many to be listed. The similarities yet to be defined. Similarities? No feel. No touch. Yet they both hunger, both weep, both run for their daily bread – one out of need, the other for fulfillment, for achievement, for the better things in life. They all love, they all breed, they all breathe the same air. Have you ever even thought that the air around touches all? You, me, then you again. It stretches like a connecting tissue, throbbing with life, stretching, accommodating, connecting.

You and me, us and them.

The lepers live in a group at the edge of habitation, shunned by society. They belong to neither a caste nor a creed; neither a single religious group nor any esoteric cult. They have crossed the boundaries of usual forms of recognition. They are beyond the pale of society that in its hauteur calls itself civilized.

The lepers are united, united by the formlessness of their bodies, the misery of their existence and the crass behaviour of society which believes in dumping that which it cannot hide. There are no castes, no creeds, no religions to segregate them. They have a unique identity – one in expression, one in feeling, one in pain, one in life, one in death.

The laugh, they cry, they watch people run by….. Sometimes they weep at seeing familiar faces. Faces that till yesterday held love, or at least recognition. Once dumped, once thrown, they are forgotten. Written off.

Early morning, another day, a woman cries. A new addition. Society's reject. Screaming.

The inmates wake up to her cries. Many go to her. Some watch from the sidelines. The same old story, nothing new. The same old tragedy, nothing new. The old woman hid her patches, hid her loss of sensation for fear of condemnation. But with the passage of time, she failed to hide her shifting features – the loss of her beauty till then divine. How could they bear with the cursed one, how indeed? Those for whom she had toiled – morning to evening – each day and sometimes even at night.

Bholu sniggered. The same old story, the same old bottle, the same old wine. On one pretext or the other society gets rid of those it cannot digest, of those it cannot hide. The old, the infirm, the weak, the weakened. What we cannot stomach, cannot define, cannot understand, cannot cure, we get rid of.

Those who are different suffer. Those who do not learn this are made to go through the grind. The planes may be different – the physical, the professional, the mental, the moral, the spiritual – the result, the reaction is the same. Shut your eyes.

For how long, for how long indeed. The pigeon

shut its eyes to wish away the approaching cat. The consequence? It died.

A people, a race, which exists on make believe loses touch with reality. The rot settles in, the crumbling begins. The decay rampant, firefighting, rosy pictures – create only patch work. See this, hide that. Believe this, not that.

And we believe. After a point do we have a choice? The problem multiplies. The will to change trembling against gusts of wind either dies or retreats to safety behind.

The solution? Simple. Acknowledge the truth. Comprehend it in totality. A hand that is bruised, an eye that is black, cannot smile at the feet which are not.

Today arms are amputated, teeth broken. But, no. Do not look at them. Look at the back, the stomach. Oh! So robust so fine.

Wake up to reality for reality has a way of its own. But still if you must close your eyes – remember the pigeon, remember the cat.

Bholu sniggered as he started his day. Bholu sniggered at all things these days. Bholu even sniggered at the thoughts in his mind.

The ways of this life were strange for Bholu. Bholu had been a mediocre lad, a mediocre person, living from moment to moment. Life progressed and so did the disease which now held his body a prisoner in its tight grip. Bholu, unaware, did not pay heed. His parents were too busy keeping body and soul together to bother. His father sold vegetables while his mother worked in those big houses, washing dishes and clothes. His father was a drunkard and his mother a woman so deep in her sorrows that she was quite oblivious of her children.

Bholu and the other children were left to fend for themselves. Their aches, pains and happiness were their own as there was often no one to share them with at home. Bholu, the eldest child, had only the younger siblings for company. They were more of a responsibility than anything else.

And so after a few years, Bholu's disease took telltale signs. His mother noticed, at long last, the cursed imprints on his features. She tried hard to help him. Bholu knew that she had tried. She had worked harder than ever to buy him the cure; she had toiled longer and longer to foil fate's design.

All these years Bholu's mother had thought that her misery would end when Bholu, her eldest son, would grow up and shoulder the burden of running the house and marrying off his sisters. Yet, now, Bholu had only added to her burdens.

Bholu's discomfort increased. His feeling mind recognized the misery of his mother's existence. She was keeping up a brave face, dismissing curious gazes while she worried for him and for the fate of her daughters whom she would find difficult to settle if the reality got into circulation.

So, one night as they all slept, Bholu walked away hiding the sound of his movements under the cover of his father's drunken babbling. He walked away... and slinking through the city in time reached here. He was now a member of this community amidst whom he felt accepted. His changing form did not matter, his plight did not seem pitiable and he was no longer a bother. He was not gawked at, nor did he feel repulsive. They were all the same. This thought worked like balm on his soul. His mind had learnt to live with the rest, to find security in this faceless, nameless, amorphous identity. It was strange but he felt secure in the midst of more of his kind. Strangely secure. No hurt, no pain. Acceptance – total – unquestioned.

Chora and Shera were fighting again. They were the most violent of the lot. The pests. They often destroyed the peace around. Loud hollering sounds emanated today from their direction. No one bothered. It was almost a daily occurrence.

People went about their chores, pottering about, busy without business. Yes. Life encompasses all that is around, the mundane and the sublime. Bholu was stitching his trousers; needle and thread counting each step on their way to repair the tear. Bholu stuck in life's routine longed for the decay of his mind. His mind that was still alert, still throbbing, still vividly recalling his family left behind, just a few miles away. Not so distant...yet out of reach. What had happened, he wondered, to his mother, his sisters, his little brother.... He grimaced as the needle pierced the stub of his finger. He grimaced not at the pain, for there was none, but at the sight of blood oozing out of lifeless fingers, dripping down and collecting in little pools near his formless feet.

A shriek! Had his mouth let it off without his mind knowing? Was this a new stage of degradation? A sigh of relief left his thankful lips as he realized it was young Surma, Shera's neighbour, shrieking.

His eyes followed the sound to rest on the flapping polythene roof of Shera's so called home. Surma, white as ash, was pointing to the torn tatters of jute that flew with the wind below the dirty polythene covering which passed for a roof.

Some saw and looked away unimpressed. Some walked up to see what was going on, and then the commotion started. The sound grew louder and louder. Almost everyone was speaking at once. Almost everyone was gesticulating fiercely. It was quite a sight to see a band of lepers so agitated.

Painfully Bholu dragged himself to Shera's so called home. The mumblings and rumblings, the shrieks, the shouts gave away a lot. Bholu learnt that Shera had been stabbed. Blood was oozing out from his wounds. He had bled to death. Bholu looked at his finger and sighed.

Bholu's mind was playing tricks again. He saw

himself sprawled on the floor, bleeding through his finger, waiting to bleed, bleed and bleed till death released him. He was suffering, his heart was aflutter but his mind was active. His mind cursed him for the day he had walked away from his mother. His being shuddered wishing for the touch of his mother, wishing her by his side. His mind wondered and raised a thousand questions mocking him for his lack of answers. Bhôlu broke into a sweat as he recovered from his vision. He shrank away as the familiar routine started. The body, or whatever was left of it, was dragged, pulled by the limbs held by gloved hands. The sweepers were paid to do the job of disposing such dead bodies by the Municipality. These fellows who were deeply intoxicated pulled Shera like one would a dog. Hah! maybe not even a dog these days!

Then Shera was thrown unceremoniously into a handcart, covered carelessly with a gunny sack, tied down with rope and pulled away. No pomp, no show, no ceremony. When the end comes it is as degrading as the life which went before it.

Bholu's mind was restless, it kept asking him Why? Why should he suffer such a fate when he had a mother, a brother and sisters still alive. That his end could be around the corner, that anybody in this group could be dead the next moment was a tangible reality.

Bholu talked to himself and repeated his justifications. His heart shrank back regretfully but his mind refused to comply. His mind kept telling him to go back to his home and ensure a proper life and possibly a decent death. He slept to turn it off. But it kept awake. The body slept restlessly, but the mind which was stubborn single-mindedly created pictures. Pictures of his mother weeping for him wondering about his health. Pictures of his sisters lost in thoughts about him.

Bholu woke up before daybreak. He pottered around. Days passed but his condition remained the same. Shera's end had jolted him badly and his mind played tricks again and again. Until he gave in unknowingly, until he believed in the pictures created by it. Until he forgot about how the walls divided the us and the them.

Bholu started living in a make-believe world which was all a creation of his overactive mind. He almost smelt his mother's cooking, he almost hugged her tonight. He felt her presence next to him as if she was sleeping by his side.

Bholu awoke a few hours later. He took out his clothes and put them on slowly, lost in thought. He went to get new bandages and then he decided to re-explore. He walked down the lanes in pain yet his whole being felt alive. His heart leapt at every familiar sight and he responded to the ambience on each side. He hobbled on his way, eager steps measuring the miles. "Oh!" he thought, "why had I not done it earlier, why not indeed?"

At last he saw the place where he was born. A joyful sigh escaped his lips. He wondered whether his mother was inside. He walked up with a confidence which was entirely the creation of his mind. He was at the boundary wall when he saw his mother walk out. She was busy with the broom, dusting things around. She had frayed over the years, but Bholu thanked the heavens that she was still alive.

She looked around with unseeing eyes and then her eyes fell on Bholu. As she looked at him, his heart beat loud, so loud that he felt that everybody could hear it. And then it shrank as it saw no sign of recognition in her manner and no emotion touch her face. Bholu's heart sank and so, probably, did his face. And then, in an instant, he recognized the puzzled recognition as she glanced deep into his eyes. He waited, almost rooted, expecting her to run and pull him into her arms and cover all the distances between them with a joyful leap.

But she did no such thing. She turned away slowly, her manner rejecting. Her rejection, which was instantaneous, was total and absolute. It crushed Bholu totally and entirely.

The exhaustion of all these years enveloped him in an instant. The shame and remorse engulfed him. He slipped into the bylane weeping silent tears. His stupidity at the dream reunion was exposed naked before his gaze. He shrank from the sight. How could he have imagined anything like that? Anything like that at all.

He came back in a daze to his tattered hut. He felt regret that was deep, so deep that his heart writhed in pain. His mother, his very own flesh and blood had rejected him... Flesh and blood? That which had been melting away, had always been melting away? Like life itself... melting each moment, from moment to moment, unheard, unfelt, unsung.

Bholu looked at his arms, at his feet, and touched his cheeks. Yes, what mattered were only these. These and none else! A heart of gold, a deep soul...who cared for them? None at all, for these cannot be seen.

Life reeked of disintegration. From mother to son from one to one, from part to part, from body to soul.

Dragging himself around, Bholu was aware of the vision flashing before him. The letting down, the obvious rejection, the loss of hope. Hope? Yes, hope of love, of acceptance – visions that his mind had conjured up again and again.

Bholu sank to the floor and remained inert for hours. His tears had died with his hope. His vision of a happy reunion, of sipping tea in the sun, of dying amongst loved ones, was blown away like ashes in the wind.

Days passed as he pottered around his hut. His mind, that tricky piece of flesh, was cast aside. His visions, all his dreams, had been untrue; they had truly misled him. The reality which lay at hand, which he had ignored for the yesterday past as much as his longing for a future tomorrow, now gave meaning to his life. For the first time he saw the world around him clearly. For the first time he saw the lepers as people. People who suffered like him, people who were shunned like him, people who had a lot of sorrow and pain to share like him. Something in him had kept him away, something had pulled him back. But, today was different, today was really different. His body felt alive, real. He felt an eagerness for the days and a longing for the nights. Life had been harsh, life had been kind too. He felt the sun warming his heart and with a renewed will, he stepped out into the world. He worked to forge friendships with his acquaintances. He wanted to take care of them, and receive whatever they could give in return – a whimper, the wag of the tail, or even hope....

Hope of love, hope of joy, hope of togetherness. From then on, Bholu, mixed with all around, cheered them, cajoled them, held them, fed them.

Till the end he lived a better human being sharing

sorrow, pain and love. Finally, he died one day and saw his limp form beneath. He saw the carcass being shifted and dumped, yet he felt no pain. That which he had nurtured, that which he had gained, was with him still. And now he could clearly see that that end was really no end.

HAUNTING LEGACY

Billu was a young boy at the tender age of seven. He loved moving around in the Mohalla. His house was the centre of his small world and for his father and mother he was the light of their eyes.

Billu, in his confused innocence, would say that he loved his father more than his mother in one instant and, that he loved his mother more than his father in the next. But what Billu loved at all times was running around like the train that he had seen at the station not so long ago. Chugga chugga – chugga chugga. Heh heh heh. His innocent laughter would bring smiles to the most rigid of faces. The labourers returning after a hard day in the fields would join in his playful banter and momentarily forget the drudgery of their existence.

Billu's unceasing chatter would often drive his mother crazy. His babbling, his running after make believe fairies all over the fields, and his preoccupation with trains would exhaust her so much that she would sleep like a log through the night.

The pressures of running a huge farming establishment and that of running a home ensured that Rani, Billu's mother, woke up early with the rooster about to announce the break of dawn. She was on her toes monitoring the huge army of farm labourers and the many others in her husband's employment from morning till evening. Rani's husband was a rich man with huge land holdings. However, he was also a keen businessman who was often too busy to devote time to farming. Therefore the responsibility of running the huge farm fell on Rani's shoulders, who fulfilled this with such devotion that she ran the farm and the house with clockwork perfection. The cozy picture that arose warmed the hearts of all those who knew the family well enough to peek into the inner portals of their life.

Like all fairy tales that have the proverbial witch hiding in the shadows to upset the well laden apple cart of the fairy godmother, Rani's heart used to dread the evil eyes that the less fortunate used to cast upon her well being. To ward off any mishap, Rani would regularly try to propitiate all the gods and goddesses and seek their blessings.

Yet the feeling of uneasiness would dog her off and on. It was a feeling similar to the one she had years ago as a child of seven, while protecting her dress from getting soiled during her birthday party.

She remembered crying unconsolably when it had. She also remembered forgetting her sorrow when her father had got her another one. But, today, her fears were difficult to put at rest. For, today, the happy ambience that surrounded her was irreplaceable.

Billu had been suffering from fever for the past few days and was uncharacteristically cranky. It was just one of those days. He was throwing all that his hands could reach in the midst of a fantastic temper tantrum. His tantrum was due to the absence of Monu, the cat who had played train-train with him the previous evening. Babli, the maid, tried to play train-train but it was beyond her capabilities and, probably, also beyond her calling. The poor girl had tried to replace Monu herself only to receive a whack on her back.

Amidst all the cajoling and crying sounded a siren... the unmistakable moaning sound, which more often than not brought unwelcome news.

Rani's heart fluttered uncontrollably as the siren grew louder and all thoughts that its path would wind away from her house and that she would not fall in the path of misfortune were proved wrong. A small prayer escaped her lips just as the police ambulance creaked to a halt.

Rani ran to the doorstep amidst stunned silence as the body of her husband was thrown on the porch by the constables. She was aghast to see his skull open and his brain exposed. She saw his stony eyes and his tongue hanging out. A gory sight. She wanted to shut her eyes, she wanted to wipe the picture in front of her, she wanted to wake up from this horrible nightmare.

But she was forced to live through all this. To her it was a nightmare, a dreadful nightmare. In her dazed state she tried to wake up from it to the happiness she was enveloped in only moments ago.

But no, no, this was for real. She could hear the

voices speak – speak of her dead husband as a terrorist – a dreaded terrorist who had been shot dead in an encounter in the fields.

She wanted to cry, she wanted to shout, but all she could do was stare open-mouthed at the man who lay in front of her. Her numb frame bent slowly down to meet the dead form below. Her mind refused to admit that he was dead. Her being revolted as she tried to push the flesh back into the skull.

Rani thought to herself, Terrorist indeed! A man unarmed! A man incapable of committing the smallest crime, could he be a terrorist? And even if he was, shrieked her whole being, silently amidst sobs, who had given those wretches the right to kill him? He was all she had .... Did anyone bother? Why did they not kill her, too, when they had snuffed out her life in this manner.

Yes, who had given them the right to so misbehave. Was it the law?

Which law do they hark about? That which is broken, twisted, flaunted with impunity. Or, that which they sell day in and day out? Or that which they abuse without a thought?

Even a prostitute is better than them. She sells herself to fill her stomach but they sell on full ones. They snatch, they rape yet they escape.

Rani performed the acts that her mind revolted against. She draped her husband, she dressed him, she readied him for cremation. She did it all with the help of Ramu the old faithful servant who still remembered the debt he owed to his master. The others had all slid away breaking all bondages and all linkages.

Ramu's vacant eyes reflected the flames that leapt to the sky. Ramu's vacant manner also reflected the shadows the future held for Rani and Billu.

Rani's thoughts were morose. Was it such moments that led women to jump on the pyre? Was it the void of helplessness and vulnerability that made them decide in favour of the unknown?

These thoughts and more churned her being and brought forth emotions Rani had never thought to exist in her bosom. Her tears dried on her cheeks and her thoughts turned from her husband's lit pyre to her son whom she found in a state of shocked delirium in Babli's lap.

Babli watched over Billu like a fierce terrier. The turn of events had been equally painful for her. Today, as the father figure of the household lay dead she had refused to let her eyes weep. Babli believed that only cowards weep not people of substance, at least not when they are in public.

And so Babli carried herself with the same poise and confidence that had been her identity ever since the day she had set foot in this house as a maid to Billu.

Billu was too young to comprehend the dimensions

of death and the gravity of the loss that was his, but he was old enough to understand the solemnity of the occasion. He was old enough to retain in his mind's eye the horrible picture of his father in tatters and recollect his mother's sobs. He was old enough to feel Ramu's vacant eyes.

An unknown fear raised its head in his heart and made him cling in his delirium to Babli. Babli and Billu had both sought refuge in the room to the side away from the sorrowful proceedings only to be drawn into a vortex of emotions, shutting the eyes yet unable to shut the mind.

Billu had heard about terrorists. But that his Bapa was a terrorist? How come he never knew? He had asked his grandmother, Nano, about death when the sparrow had died. Nano had said that things go to heaven when they die. And today it was Bapa. But why was he torn apart? Why were Bapa's clothes so dirty when he went to see God? His Bapa had always worn clean clothes before he met people. Had Bapa forgotten...had Bapa forgotten.... And when would he come back?

Billu drifted from thought to thought in delirium. In his delirium he heard his mother's voice. Now he waited for it to fade and be replaced by another thought, but his mother's voice grew louder and louder till he could bear it no more and he screamed his way to wakefulness. His mother was shaking him like a leaf. It was only after a while that she realized that her son had woken up.

As she clung to him, her sorrow, her concern was communicated to Billu with every touch and look. For seven year old Billu, for whom his parents and his surroundings had been the things he had learnt to identify with till that moment, life seemed a burden.

What is a seven year old? Does he deserve the absence of a father forced on him by circumstances beyond his control? Does he deserve to see his mother, a pillar of strength and source of joy, turn sorrowful? Does he deserve to see life as more than an opportunity to fly like the bees or hum like the birds.

Life decides what it gives to whom and why it takes away what it does. No questions are asked no answers given. Some call it fate, some destiny. Yet others say it is the will of God. Yet others may say what God? You reap as you sow.

Whatever you or they say or think, life is a dream, life is hell, life is different again and again. Life changes colour without a murmur. It a game of touch and go and till you know, its often too late.

Life is like the food in the orphange – never good to eat yet difficult to forgo. Life is a myth, a burden, and an opportunity. We live and plan for year and years, oblivious of the maker and his writ. We love and we hate. We lay traps and we wait. We hunt for reality, we search for meanings, forgetting to acknowledge the greatest truth – the temporariness of it all.

Why are we here? Why do we come wailing, live, breed, die. Why? Why? O Why? Why did the maker send us here to struggle? To succeed? To kill? To amass treasures? Think.... Think... think.... To whom does it matter who you are? To whom does it matter what you did? To whom does it matter whether you gave alms or begged? To whom indeed?

To none but you yourself. To none but you yourself.

And when the end comes, so will the memories of all the things you did. It matters not what you leave behind as much as what you take with you. It matters not how you lived but, yes, it matters how you died.

Babli smiled at Billu. Because of her poise, to Billu she seemed to be the only one untouched by the goings-on in the house. For Billu her familiar manner was the biggest reassurance and cause of hope of things returning to normal again.

Days passed and become months. The months slipped into years. Time weighed heavily on the shoulders of Rani, Billu and Babli. Ramu, the old faithful was still around. On their shoulders Billu and his mother carried the burden of his father's misfortune. That Billu was a terrorist's son was reason enough for being ridiculed and looked down upon. Billu silently cursed the day his father was shot as a terrorist.

From a carefree lad Billu had become a responsible one. From the apple of the eye of his parents he had become the butt of criticism and jokes for others. Billu often wanted to give it all up and to escape. But, Billu could not escape, if only for the sake of his mother.

Billu knew that he was the only reason why his mother still lived from day to day, bravely facing the curses and taunts of her neighbours. Billu had known that his mother was a strong woman but that she was this strong was a revelation to him. Billu often wondered at her strength and also wondered whether it was the adversity that left her with no choice but to be strong? Billu had seen the fire in her eyes, the fire of purpose, the fire of revenge, the fire of expectation.

Rani had faith in life and strongly believed that all things change. No seasons are permanent, all things change.

She had suffered each day, a hopeful lonely woman waiting for the promised change.

Billu fired by the purpose of her expectations single-mindedly pursued the course his mother had outlined for him. With the passage of time, Billu grew up into a promising, handsome young man. He had his goals clearly in view.

Of course, there were diversions as always since his life was still in its youth. Despite his maturity in most matters, some emotions were beyond his control. Emotions which till now had been remorseful, regretful, baneful now started changing colour in the spring of his life. Like a breeze of fresh air shares its fragrance with the dark dim and dank corners when the windows are thrown open, so also young Billu's heart experienced the bliss of joy when Shalini's presence enlivened his mundane existence. Shalini was in the same class as Billu. She also happened to be the only child of the local prince who was known to be a very fair and just human being.

For Rani, however, Billu was still the same young boy who was carrying the burden of their misfortune, a boy who was also carrying the burden of her expectations. For Rani, Billu was the only one who could set the record straight. He was the only one who could prove that his veins did not carry the blood of a terrorist. By living an exemplary life he would have to prove that his father was not a terrorist, that he had been only named a terrorist. For Rani this was a necessity, a passion, and a burning desire.

Billu, who bore the brunt of taunts and the adversity of times as well as the change in men and friends on his tiny shoulders at first unknowingly, then painfully, increasingly became an introvert. He was a boy who heard everyone speak but spoke little himself, a boy, who with time had learnt that he could say much but no one would believe.

When times are favourable, all is well. When times are bad, people crush even the mighty into dust. That times were really bad had been his experience. That people had danced on the graves of dead men. That they had drunk from their skulls. He had also learnt that these were the signs of weak men. The strong fight face to face and embrace the results of their actions. The weak wait patiently; they wait till the end – like vultures waiting to feast on a carcass.

Often Billu felt as though he was a hundred years old. Life had so filled his existence with pain and he had learnt to live with that. Every moment seemed endless.

Yet in the presence of Shalini, Billu felt young and

carefree, forgetting within those moments the who, the why and the wherefore of his existence. He was beginning to respond to the new tremors in his life, tremors which held the promise of joy and bliss.

Billu had seen beautiful things and learnt that they were mostly beyond his reach. But this once life was treating him differently. Shalini, a bubbling stream of youthful energy, was often drawn, despite herself, to the cool calmness of Billu's presence. This once, Billu wanted to forget what he had learnt. This once Billu wanted to not merely see and appreciate silently. This once Billu desired to possess the object of his desire. He had initially thought this to be impossible and had even convinced himself. Yet, with time, his resolve was much weakened, unable to withstand the daily hammering it received from within and without.

Shalini was a beautiful girl. She signified and represented all that Billu longed for. A name, a lineage, respect, a carefree blissful existence of gaiety and mirth. She was everything that Billu felt he lacked.

She was drawn to him, as much as he was to her. The only difference was one of visibility. She was openly smitten, he….it was difficult to tell.

The years together at college passed and when it was nearing time to say good bye, pangs of deep emotion so gripped Billu that his calmness was disturbed. He was desperate to tell her all he wanted, desperate to communicate. Each night he would practice in detail what he would say. Each morning he would wait but only to let the days slip by, one by one, in tongue tied silence. Yet, Shalini knew what Billu wanted to say. Such is the power of true emotion that it overcomes physical inability whatever its cause. Shalini knew, and so did her close friends, but pride would not allow her to acknowledge or encourage him. She knew Billu like none other, yet she wanted him to speak the words she knew he was incapable of. Yes, she had heard his being resonate with hers, shrieking out the truth, yet for want of proof she had left things alone waiting for Billu to speak.

And with time the days, already numbered, came to an end. It was finally the day when the college closed. A yearly occurrence, but for Billu this was worse than death. There would be no reopening for them. Where would he find her? Where could he see her? He was so used to the daily brush with her that he was at a loss to understand what he would do with life without her.

In extreme moments, extreme actions become possible. Billu walked up to Shalini in front of all and sundry and proclaimed his love for her. He proclaimed it in the only manner possible. Loud and clear.

The result. An awkward Shalini gaped at him, then at the smiling faces all around and before she could register the full import of this new development, the words uttered by him had reached far and wide.

Shalini's father, the great prince of high lineage

was aghast. His daughter and that Billu! What else? He decided to put a stop to this at once.

Shalini... who bothered to ask her what she wanted. Billu... who thought about him as a young boy whose heart also sang songs of love. Billu was that dreaded terrorist's son. He was to be shunned. He could be good at many things. He could have his merits but these were not capable of washing away the one fact that clouded his existence.

To Shalini, it was of no consequence. She had known and loved the young Billu. To her his past had no meaning. She had loved what she knew and she could not concern herself with what was irrelevant. Love is a deep emotion. It forgives, it ennobles. It raises the standard of life itself. The love that Shalini felt for Billu was capable of forgiving him a dozen wrongs what to say of a happening beyond his control.

But Billu knew otherwise. He knew that Shalini's

father would succeed in once again raising the bogey of his parenthood to snatch away from him that which would have been his had he not been branded as a terrorist's son.

But no. This once Billu wanted to snatch from life the reason for his life. He made up his mind. He walked the distance to Shalini's house. He walked upto the man who was capable of spoiling it all and before he could do any such thing he confronted him – confronted him with his soul in his eyes. Shalini's father was a fierce man, a tall heavily built well dressed person but to Billu's eyes, blinded by his tears, Shalini father was only an insurmountable wall between him and her.

Whatever Billu's weakness, his strengths were innumerable. With age and experience the old man could understand Billu's disposition. He saw and felt his pain. Billu's father had been a contemporary of his. His heart went out to Billu, he wanted to hold him and relieve him of the tortures no man his age deserved. He moved towards him. At that instant Shalini's mother appeared in the doorway. She clutched the curtains as soon as her eyes rested on Billu. The cursed one. How could she ever allow him to marry her Shalini. How indeed? And how would she live with taunts falling her way. Those around would never spare her the barbs of poison. They would taunt Shalini, they would call them veiled names... how could she respond with the taint on her daughter's name?

No. She would not allow this to happen. No. Shalini, her only child, certainly deserved a better future. She turned and walked inside. Shalini stopped her and wanted to ask her the reason for her stand. Ma. Shalini's first spoken intelligible words had always managed to twist her insides. But today when Shalini tried her tricks, her resolve to refuse increased.

A stubborn Shalini stomped inside. The father, a helpless witness of events turned away from Billu, crushed. Amazed at the turn of events a dazed Billu walked away, unmindful of the tears flowing from his eyes falling freely by the wayside.

Many years passed. Rani and Billu had moved to the city. Billu's life achieved the dimensions Rani had prayed for. As a successful sahib he became a known figure. Power and money mould the minds of men. As Billu achieved these, people forgot his flaws. The same people began to fawn on him again. They could fool almost everyone but not Billu. For he had seen life. He was no novice to the games it played. He was no novice to the tricks it showed. Now Billu had learnt to forgive these people who were the victims of their thoughts. Their minds created images and tricked them into taking postures he now laughed at. Billu had a heart big enough to forgive but he could not forget. He had risen above his sufferings due to circumstances. He had risen above his sufferings due to expectations. The expectation to be loved by others, the expectation to be respected by others, the expectation to be revered by them.

He, Billu, a terrorist's son had learnt now to have no expectations from others, no expectations from circumstances. He had learnt the bitter truth that only life can teach. He had learnt to live a day at a time, from moment to moment, in a selfless manner, in the manner of a *karmayogi*.

Today people sought him, yesterday they had shunned him. Had he changed? Had they changed? None but perceptions had changed. To base our happiness on the expected acts of others is the biggest folly we commit repeatedly in life. The biggest folly life makes us commit each time. If ever we humans learn this truth our lives would truly be worth living.

Billu lived a full life, a life of bliss. The bliss of such an existence cannot be described in words.

But what happened to Shalini? She went her way to fulfill her own destiny. Shalini, the person who ignited the thought process of Billu, lived a life of normalcy. She was never to learn that in Billu's self realization she had played a crucial role.

THE LEGEND OF TARA

Tara felt alien with all this finery. She was feeling irritable with the heavy jewellery on her person. It was weighing down her body just as the thoughts in her mind were weighing down heavily on her soul. Tara was getting married today, of her own will, or so it seemed to the world around. The truth was far from this happy picture she was trying to paint and put forth for her widowed mother and the world to see. Her husband to be, who was from Delhi, was a powerful man. Yet she was unable to like him as a bride should.

Tara was used to running around gaily like a mountain goat without fetters. Tara was a young girl, beautiful, pampered. She lived by the side of the mountain near the stream. Bubbly and vivacious, she was the living joy of the huge family to which she belonged.

Tara used to chatter incessantly, used to run about unhindered. She had a long list of uncles and aunts who doted on her and a large following of cousins – brothers and sisters – who adored her. Theirs was a simple existence filled with the twinkling of stars and the gay shining glow of happiness. A warm light enveloped the happy family in its fold from morning till night. Tara had a way of her own which was endearing in its magnetism. She pulled people towards her like a strong shaft of light in a dark room.

Her mother thought of her as a gift from her God, the God to whom she had prayed day and night for many many years.

Tara's father was the village elder of this village located in the far eastern part of the country. For his tribe his word was law. All those who lived within the village respected him. He decided all disputes and wielded wide and absolute power over his flock.

He smoked a cigarette quietly, sitting by the side of the winding path going to the top of the mountain, as he watched the peaceful scene below. Perched on his favorite ledge, his distinctive coat and hat – signs of recognition by the British – in place, he looked with loving eyes at the cluster of bamboo huts, smoke rising from the roofs.

The next instant he jumped up with a start as a wolf howled next to him. Relief swept over him when he turned to find Tara. Tara burst out laughing on having achieved success in her design to startle her father.

Tara's status in her village was not that of the village elder's daughter. No. Tribal society recognizes no such claims.

She had an identity of her own which needed no clutches for support or help.

Tara looked down from the ledge and felt a strange glow of pride at the scene below. The light in her father's eyes shone powerfully igniting her own. What a beautiful scene it was, to one, to all, to anyone who bothered to look at it all.

Tara's father used to visit the district headquarters frequently due to his dealings with the officials the British government had sent there. They gave him a lot of gifts like clothes, cigarettes and paper money. Most of these things were useless for the villagers but still due to curiosity the whole village used to gather in the clearing to see the stuff after the arrival of the village elder.

On his return from one such visit, a handsome

young Indian from the plains had accompanied Tara's father back. He was dressed like the British and was smoking a cigarette. The girls had giggled. Was he a gift too? they mumbled as they waited for an introduction. But Tara's father was pensive, withdrawn. The fellow was shown to a shack while Tara's father went straight to his hut. It was surprising that there were no introductions. No introductions at all.

Tara's father was silently morose for days. He was thoughtful. The firangi's had twisted his arm and threatened dire consequences if he did not allow their representative, the fellow from the plains, to review his administration of the village on their behalf.

A review was unheard of, even the erstwhile Raja had never done this. The village elder's authority over his people could not be questioned by any one living, and a review – a review? He had tried to resist but pressures and threats forced him to acquiesce after being locked up in jail for three days without food, without water and without the stuff which made lights dance in front of his eyes. Smack they called it. Smack. The powder which he had been made to get used to by the officious people who had interacted with him at the headquarters. Like most of his kind he was used to smoking ganja but the powerful powder that he had got used to now was like nothing he had come across in his life earlier. It was a powder for which he could do almost anything for his body craved for it. This powder was supplied to him, subject to his good behaviour, by the headquarters. He knew he was a prisoner, a prisoner due to his addiction. Free to roam around yet forced to come back regularly for the white powder – the powder formed the chains around him, fettered him. None knew his trauma not even Tara's mother because it had happened so quickly. He had been waiting at the headquarters to meet the officials when he had been offered a cigarette to smoke. Since the moment he had smoked the cigarette, which was laced with the powder, he had graduated from one stage to another. He had been left with no room to understand the happenings till the treachery was in place.

A review? He smoked fiercely. A review! He drank more wine....Tara watched her father behave like a mad man and shrugged her shoulders. She cried within her mind. What had overcome him she wondered...was it the witch that people dreaded? The witch in the mountains. A few days later, she ran all the way to the local medicine man. She explained her worries, the old man smiled. A daughter's worries, a daughter's apprehensions. He knew what affected him. It was the slight to his pride. It was the treachery. The questioning of his authority. The questioning of his rights. A fall from grace in front of those whom he had ruled. Ruled with the love and feelings of a father, a patriarch.

Tara clutched the string of strange beads the witch doctor gave her. She ran back and put it on her father's ailing arm. She watched like a hawk waiting for his recovery. But he only deteriorated. Slowly and surely decaying in front of her eyes. She then looked at her mother wondering what to do. The mother chanted prayers, burnt leaves did all that she knew.

When all failed, they sat outside their hut, knowing, feeling, recognizing what lay in store for them. Each suffering alone in agony. Fear stopping the rush of words, hope holding them back in their tracks.

The inevitable happened. Slowly but surely, death danced over life to snuff it out fully from the heavily heaving body of the village elder. He died a slow painful death. Life seemed to fight and try desperately to win over death. For how long? Only for a passing moment, a painful moment. Life, a temporary bubble, has to burst. It wobbles over time uncertain, sometimes it swells in mistaken pride and a false sense of reality – the very act which leads it to burst.

Bubbles burst, then they form again. Each radiates the light of its maker. Those who burst and go are seldom remembered for long, seldom missed for long. Often it is said that people cry for what they lose not for those who have left. Probably yes, the material over the spiritual, the actual over the factual.

Tara and her mother had been inconsolable. They had cried and cried and turned to stone. Each passing day etched its lines on their faces and, unknown to them, criss-crossed those of their fate.

Slowly and painfully mother and daughter learnt the bitter lessons of life. Tara's gay carefree nature learnt life and living could bring misery. She saw power change hands as a new village elder was appointed by the people as per traditions but approved by the nominee of the headquarters. During her father's administration of the village affairs, each and everyone had freedom and equal opportunity to grow. But, now things were changing and changing very fast. Now she saw herself as a wretched girl, a pitiable girl, who had fallen in esteem. She began to feel suspicious of those around and her heart learnt to doubt. She changed slowly but surely from a gay carefree girl to a gawky teenager with mistrust in her eyes. The pain of life has to be endured. One cannot will it away. Talismans and chants cannot change fate. Each person has to live alone, surely and truly, right till the end.

And so Tara's life was beginning to change. It would soon change from the smooth sailing she had known since birth, to the rocky, stony passage surrounded by vultures and hounds that she was treading on these days.

Yet, all roads have trees, full of fruit and shade. In some places they are few and far between, at others there are orchards on both sides. Her path ran into rough weather but life is amazing. With each passing day, the rocky path seemed better. She seemed to be getting used to the new way with time.

A girl like Tara had a charm and beauty all her

own and despite fate's treachery and her own tattered clothes, she was still the most magnetic presence in the village.

Yet her beauty too seemed to be a curse. Such was the turn of her fate. Like a pot of unguarded gold, like an orchard without a fence, like a river without a bed, she was unsafe and at the mercy of those who took a fancy to her.

Tara's mother and Tara realized the precarious state they were in when one evening, as Tara rushed home from the stream as daylight receded, she was accosted by the British emissary who had made menacing advances towards her.

Tara had cried, loudly, but all had turned deaf. No one had ventured out as the emissary had dared to cross her path. She had pushed him out of the way with all the strength of her anger and rushed home trembling.

Tara was not the same for a long time. The lewd

eyes of the stranger followed her all around. She learnt to hate those lustful glares.

Shortly, the emissary approached the new people who were in command for Tara's hand in marriage. Seeing a wonderful opportunity to get rid of a potential nuisance that Tara was to them they talked her mother into acquiescence. Tara, the free flowing rivulet used to unhindered ways was to now force her flow to match and please others – people who had not mattered before but who now held the key to her future.

She said yes, when she wanted to say no. She smiled while her being cried. She jabbered while her self endured a slow silent mourning. She was doing it for her mother, she was doing it for the village, she was doing it for her respectability. And what she was doing was not new. No, it was not new at all.

Almost all humans compromise. They weigh the pros and cons of the available situation and decide –

some with the heart, some by position, some with the mind. For the rest circumstances decide.

And so Tara had followed the man whom she had wedded – the man from the plains, the British emissary – to the town, loaded in finery on that fateful day. Uncomfortable. Unsure. Alien. She was escorted by laughing women into the mansion which she presumed to be her husband's residence. She was left alone in a big room. Her husband came, stayed the night and left early the next day. When she awoke she found herself alone. Night turned to day and days stretched into nights blurring the memory of months and years. Slowly Tara realized that she had been sold to the Madam of the mansion, Sharbati and the man who had married her had done it to teach her a lesson for not responding to his advances. Tara was left with no options and so she did not resist as she was initiated into the lifestyle of a prostitute on the kotha of Madam Sharbati.

Years passed. A betel chewing Tara laden in

jewellery and heavy silk now commanded her own on the very kotha where her husband had left her. A gleam in the eye, a song on the lips and an ability to hold customers hostage to the feminine guiles of her lot had earned her name and fame in the most notorious red light area of the capital city.

Men loaded with money, drink in hand, and lust in their eyes were welcomed with open arms. Tara had embraced destiny and now spat in its face. Not for her were the deep dungeons of self pity or sorrow. The thought that the purest of blood flowed in the gutters and multiplied often made her laugh. Most of her clientele was well respected. The exterior was enviable but what lay beneath was repulsive. She found it amusing that some of whom she was even now entertaining were high born; they belonged to the most respectable strata of the city.

Tara had learnt early enough that life on the kotha is for those who can grab. She could now easily tell the financial worth of anyone who stepped on her doorstep in the time it takes to snap your fingers.

Tara had her favourites, but she never played favourites. Her business was strictly for money.

As the years had passed, the legend of Tara had become immortalized in folklore. Her beauty, her charm, her guile were raised much above reality and her status was that of an apsara – heavenly and often divine.

The real Tara doomed to the mortal world, aged over the years, losing slowly the characteristics of youth one by one. Tara had clutched helplessly at each one of them only to realize that like the sands of time they had slipped out of her closed fist leaving only emptiness behind.

This emptiness resounded in the hollow existence she was leading. Each moment echoed and shook her soul. She would rave and rant. She would dress up only to hate the dolled up hag who stared back at her from the mirror. She was leading a painful life, fretting and crying for that which would never be hers.

Tara,...Tara,...where was the real Tara. Is this reality or was that reality. Or are all these myths, myths all around, reality nowhere. Tara threw away the glass from which she drank. Her mind was playing tricks with her often these days. She almost felt as if her husband's face had filled the glass, eyes full of remorse and his being shattered into a sorrowful pose seemingly seeking forgiveness.

She picked up the bottle of scotch and drank herself senseless, wiping away the traces of anything else except the myth or reality that was Tara. Tara the woman who was lusted for by men and hated by their women.

Life progressed, she often felt that death was round the corner. These thoughts of death often made her look back at the path she had travelled. There was love, there was hate, there was anguish, there was praise, there was youth and, yes, now there was death.

She looked at her anger, she looked at her anguish. She looked at her suffering self as a discarded newly wed. She remembered the curses she had rained on one and all. She remembered all the pain as if it was only yesterday, only yesterday. She turned her face away from the pain. As her eyes opened she saw the silhouette of a plain looking girl, one of her victims, one whom she had forced into a life which the world condemned. For the price of a few diamonds, for the price of reams of silk, she had often pushed young trusting girls into a future dark and dim.

She felt guilty for her behaviour. She knew that what was forgiveable was her helplessness not her greed, the greed that had made her force others to a life of sorrow and pain.

She rose possessed. She fell at the girl's feet. She begged forgiveness. The poor girl wanted to kick Tara, hit her, shred her to pieces. Yet the swaying body that begged her forgiveness, holding her feet in her hands, made her weep.

How could she forgive Tara, how indeed? Tara's soul was stuck in the haggard body seeking forgiveness. She was suffering immensely. The young girl looked at her with pity, and kicked her aside. No...No...No....

Tara's body gurgled and turned limp. A horrible sight. The apsara Tara, the prostitute Tara, the myth Tara, the real Tara.

Tara's limp form turned rigid and finally putrified. No one saw the decay as no one comes to visit Tara now-a-days. However, the legend of Tara which raised her beauty to that of an apsara still circulates in the capital city oblivious of her reality.